Traction Man Is Here!

MINI GREY

Dear Santa
Well I expect you know about what happened to my old Traction Man and the Terrible Parachute Accident. Well did you know there is a NEW Traction Man You can buy?

Hallo! All in a day's work!

warfare shirt

dazzle-painted battle pants

combat boots

JUNGLE

SPACE

Here is a picture of the NEW Traction Man. I know you are very busy. I hope you like this letter. SUB AQUA

ALFRED A. KNOPF

New York

Traction Man is here!
(Wearing Combat Boots,
        Battle Pants, and his
                Warfare Shirt.)

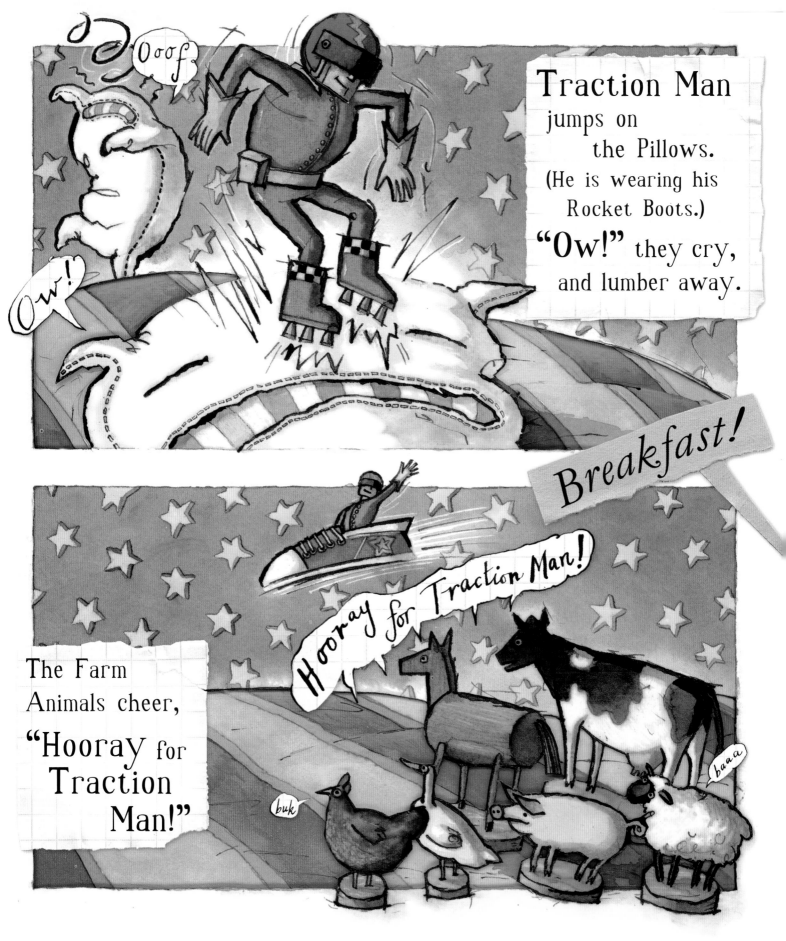

Traction Man is guarding some toast.

Now
who's going to help
with the washing up?

He volunteers for a Special Mission.

Traction Man is diving in the foamy waters
of the Sink (wearing his Sub-Aqua Suit,
Fluorescent Flippers, and Infra-Red Mask).

He is searching for the
Lost Wreck of the Sieve.

"Well done,
Scrubbing Brush!
You can be my pet!"

Traction Man is crawling through the overgrown shrubbery near the Pond, wearing Jungle Pants, Camouflage Vest and Sweaty Bandanna.

The Dollies have all been buried up to their waists in the flowerbed by Wicked Professor Spade.

"Oh, Traction Man, how can we repay you?"
"Think nothing of it, Ladies.
              All in a day's work."

Traction Man and Scrubbing Brush are
deep, deep down at the Bottom of the Bath.
(Traction Man is wearing his Deep-Sea Diving Suit,
Brass Helmet, and Metal Shoes.)
    Somewhere down here, legend says,
            are the Mysterious Toes.

Oh, no!
The Toes have
suddenly appeared
and have captured
**Scrubbing
Brush!**

"No Mysterious Toes can steal away with my brave pet! Take that! And that!"

The Toes cannot **stand** it and release Scrubbing Brush.

Traction Man takes some photographs of the Mysterious Toes.

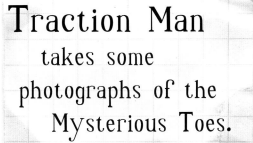

At last!
Granny's!

Everyone has a present to open.
Even **Traction Man**.

Scrubbing Brush
is **very** excited.

Oh! How lovely (grrrr).
An all-in-one knitted green romper suit
and matching bonnet!

"I knitted it myself," says Granny.
"It is special Traction Man green. For jungles."

Oh, how nice.

Socks again.

It is
a perfect
fit.

Traction Man
is speeding in his
Supersonic
Space-Cup
and Saucer
(wearing his all-in-one
knitted green romper suit
and matching bonnet)
on his way to rescue
the Cupcake from
the clutches of
Doctor Sock.

But—
Oh, no!

Well, at least Scrubbing Brush doesn't laugh at him.

Traction Man is sitting on the edge of the Kitchen Cliff
(wondering how long he will have to wear his all-in-one knitted
green romper suit and matching bonnet).

Arf Arf Arf

Arf!

Arf!

Arf!

"Oh, DO be quiet,
Scrubbing Brush."

My goodness! Down there!
 All those Spoons have crashed! They must be helped—
but how? The Kitchen Cliff is very high.

"Look at that dust cloud! We must hurry! **The Broom is coming!**"

What **IS** Scrubbing Brush doing?

Traction Man and **Scrubbing Brush**
are relaxing after their latest mission,
lying comfortably on a book
in the huge blue expanse
of the Carpet.

Traction Man is wearing his
knitted Green Swimming Pants
and matching Swimming Bonnet.

They are both wearing their medals.

And they know they are ready
for **Anything.**